Leonard Schwartz

OBJECTS OF THOUGHT, ATTEMPTS AT SPEECH

Gnosis Press • New York

An Alternate Currents Edition
Published by Gnosis Press

Some of the poems published in this volume have previously appeared in the following reviews and anthologies, to which due acknowledgment is made: *Alea, American Letters and Commentary, Asylum, Central Park, The Literary Review, Pearl, Talisman.*

Cover design by Gregory Kapelyan
Cover photograph, "Flatiron Building, Rain", 1975,
by Rudy Burckhardt

The editors gratefully acknowledge the assistance of the New York City Department of Cultural Affairs Art Apprenticeship Program.

For information, address the publisher:
Gnosis Press
P.O. Box 42
Prince Street Station
New York, New York 10012

Library of Congress Cataloging-in-Publication Data

Schwartz, Leonard 1963-
Objects of Thought, Attempts at Speech.

(Alternate currents)
I. Title.
PS3569.C5665025 1990   811-.54 -- dc20   90-3319
ISBN 0-922792-00-3   CIP

For my mother and father

CONTENTS

AS YOU RUN UP THE STAIRS

Dictionary   9
As You Run Up the Stairs   10
Ideal Speech Situation   12
Deep Season Reply   14
The Sight-Line   15
The Pier   16
Abrogations   17
Progression   21
A Question to Celan   23
Attempt at Speech   24
Art of Expectation   26
Between Perception   27

LIVING AND DYING
IN A SINGLE EXCHANGE

Poem   33
Report From Paris   34
The Beautiful American Word "Sure"   35
The Garden   37
December   38
I, It   40
Eight Variations on a Stranger   42

REAWAKENING

Awaiting Validation   47
Vulva Myth   49
Desire   51
Form   54
Meditation   55

AS YOU RUN UP THE STAIRS

Dictionary

Yesterday the dictionary scattered, fell like leaves.

Not a scattering universally attended,
nor the eclipse of scattered truths, nor
            a human scattering, of human seed.

It was a scattering of all the words that did not catch—
            and none of them did—
a fallow fantasia of language, meaning less
than any of the points of light in a planetarium

until, finally, almost unbearably,
this scattering became the world at large.

As You Run Up the Stairs

> *"I seized it and opened it, and in silence*
> *I read the first passage on which my eyes fell."*
>   - St. Augustine

Story of a garden:
in the middle of the story,
an account of the will.
Mysterious process: twisting
and turning in bronze-silver chains.
Golden reproaches, opening a book,
where the random eye falls.
The shaping of thought a difficult work,
never completed, or never begun.
Searching in thought for what you were thinking:
whirling to look when nothing is there.

Flesh, color, speech:
these exist by the rivalry
amongst little phrases.
The struggle to conceive,
sounds that palpitate and style the possible:
distant horizons that complicate a ghetto
in a grove, in the shadow of a city
that goes on writing.
Enclosing circles:
it pained and they gave me something
to quell the pain.
Searching in books for what's to be said:
whirling in thought as you run up the stairs.

The space of the mind
in constant retreat from space,
the voices we hear,
no longer coming from things.
A glance at the floor:
no rational argument can ever succeed
in calming such doubts. Yet no one
can wield these words, without adding
phantasms to the real. *The language supports the facsimile,*
ideality leaps in the hands.
Searching in thought for a way to get out:
it pained and they gave me something
to quell the pain.
Enclosing circles: twisting
and turning in bronze-silver chains.
Whirling to leave when no way is there.

Ideal Speech Situation

Corridors
arrested in buildings
fractured by doors:
hammers of a strange correction:
"drowned men, pale and thoughtful,
sometimes drifting by"
everything that has laughed or was laughable
rungs of an abandoned hatchway, wet with jam;
despair, glutting the mouth.

Can you pinpoint amongst these
a cherished image
beside the foaming pale
in the strip tide of passing services
find yourself untouched?
The films over a child's eyes
the lips of fairies
the adolescents' voices changing octaves
by the pool-side
everything that has laughed or was laughable
up on the same dais, your words and more,
afterwards, whisked away, whining...

Hope? Who can hold you back from hope?
Seriously, you blankly insist
you haven't changed, wholly altered
you stare at shores
and glow with discourse
everything that has laughed or was laughable
battering you, insinuater, you vast and leafless ceasing.
We shall not drown you but there is no need to thank me

I'm the taut rope around your past
that will hang that part of anyone
where day and night were once a solution of jots and jolts
everything that has laughed or was laughable
careening like brightly played percussion
in the bloated corridors of this penalty
crowding in these shouldered lakes
these exchanges, these exclusions
the dear dead gentle persons.

Deep Season Reply

Viscous matter got knocked from the jars
    during an unscheduled chase
After glimpsed VIP's; the sexual act came later
With each passing day. Waiting for the bittersweet
    to get less bitter
The only entertainment available was an unkind pamphlet
About a sapsucker felled by a poisoned
Tree, the whole story done in vicious humor.
Later your sideswiped finger
    directed attention to quadruplets,
Signing to us out in the street.

As desire deteriorated,
All frames of reference passing away
Into a white so blinding it pierced our eyes,
I stumbled wirelessly over the affected adjectives,
Vacuuming down original intentions, lint, and latest crumbs,
Until the room was cleaned of everything but the act itself.
A polygraph for polyglots, you finally said,
Has its reasons for flowering.

The Sight-Line

No shoreline but the sight-line,
Red "Texaco" sign on the other side of the Hudson,
Views of George Washington, of the line of lights
That stretches up the closed highway, undercut
By a second highway, where traffic hungers,
Where structures and light move to killer logic.

Dogs walk here, are walked.
There is humor in this, just as
There is humor in the rain's delay,
Just as there is humor in the wind's persistence.
The sky will push, forcing the eye to shut
Behind its umbrella, even as the bridge comes fully lit.

On such occasions you are asked to believe in directions.
In point of fact you partially assent to it.
There is direction to this force on the veins,
There is direction to this tight grip asserted on the bone.
In the assembly lines of the skull, the thing outside
Is made, and you watch it spread, and you tremble.

The Pier

In the ink-blue light, the polished stones
presumably in solar motion

might merely be a mural drying.
Bottlecaps sparkle underfoot

like eyesight fallen to earth.
Coffee spills, steaming from the ground:

its smoke is damaged. The pier is old.
Its clouds are gowned in poison.

Upon the neon signs overwhelming the sea,
onto this bark going nowhere,

tumbles, as if into a courtyard,
dry starlight and the final labor:

it is here, in this labor, that is washed and hung
the last lookout over the stream of fear.

This is the tentflap of the sea, of what is known
at a distance, as if in another key.

Abrogations

Terminus

It is a place of light
that eddies as if water,
the zero point, the terminus,
of so much strain, of thought:
to thought, the afterthought,
to life, the dying moment.
Was it worth it? And if not,
was the second "it" worth the first?
It is a place of water
that eddies as if light.

Terminal Path

To know nothing, to go on speaking.
To say nothing, to go on thinking,
looking, walking, looking.
And as you are walking
to persist in thinking—ignorantly,
silently—that words are a path,
that, therefore, this is a path.

To go on nothing.

There Is a Sudden Warmth

In your movements you feel
a sudden warmth

The places that you move
beginning to grow on you in their stillness

Like the dense outpouring of heat
from a radiator:

Yet this momentary illusion of wholeness
registers only as a quiet feeling

A ray of sun of which one feels a part
what you said in the darkened car

Warmly inviting me to reenter my life,
raising me up against your thigh.

There is a draft here
cool and hot at once—

Later, a gasp of pleasure unfolds up the body
in the well-being that the body wills be so.

(Forgotten then, that warmth grows cold,
as passing as speech.

That well-being passes as the torso tosses
the sudden warmth you feel fleeting

As among the shadows in a cave,
the afterimage of the wholly real.)

Thought

The frailty of endeavor
fuels endeavors, and the lie
is that every thought—

they occur in time, one by one,
yet all at once seem to cluster around
a central nerve;

and that every motion—
elongated in the half-light,
tawdry in the full, without
consciousness in the moving crowd,
with it in the empty room—
is not one.

Limbo

Not eternal rest but a lamp
burning among the dead,
and in the ways
we light ourselves, flesh
frames of what shredded love,
as things sweep shut,
or are opened up, and this
is our funeral, we think,
and are careful to look away.

It is the same life we are all exhausting,
wicks low. Go form it,
lisps the mud under the lid.
Bloom, reads the dark,
and we plunge blindly in again,
behind the lips and the tongue,
as if the sex were unending.
As if passion and the after-life were one.

Today the Panic Dissolves

Today the panic dissolves, resounding with life
in the downpour of light,
a voyage, a mirage, and a horizon, all.

Arousing myself to the solemnity of this radiance.
Not to branches of venturing ash.
Not to musings on watery loss.
But to the objects of this adventure,
the abrogation of all that is not real.

Progression

Mediate between the knifelike sleep of last night, and this
progression. It cannot be done. The difference is absolute.

In spite of that, a third possibility already appears over
the ridge, a possiblity as disordered as a jailbreak, as
desperate, and yet, portrayed differently, as farcical.
In any case, it is the disorder that counts, the promise of
abrupt and desirable changes, with the expectation of a new
order soon to follow: to speak of disorder is first to admit
of the dream of order, built into the territory as casually
as gravel or grass.

The idea that change will not be desirable, that in fact it
will be destructive, only rarely makes its appearance during
this phase. Destruction gains no place in the meditative chain.
Since negation must always negate the whole, not simply the
one significant gesture, and the whole cannot be negated, ever.
Seemingly implying that the destruction that one envisions
from time to time is necessarily a falsification of destruction,
that the annihilation one imagines is never related to actual
putrefaction.

But what was it that last night's sleep was trying to show me,
and showed me so successfully? Illusions parted like the surface
of a fruit, leaving a serrated edge glistening with sweet juice,
only it wasn't so much the illusions that were cut as the truths.
So that to feel for a moment, the moment just before, that the
world was completely unfathomable, beyond our capacities to
judge or think, itself was understandable. And that to feel the
contents of the mind shiver under contact with some blunt
mood was also understandable, in its moment. As if to exper-

ience our emptiness we had to know of it first, but with that knowledge, everything then were to achieve its perfect place. Yet nothingness might be falling during the night after all, like a steady rain that goes unheard since the air-conditioner is left running. That negation should breed negation hardly seems possible, and yet it happens that way, as once again you must admit to the absence of any certain feeling about whether this is or isn't a dome about to crack. The way people will rubber-neck because they don't really know what has happened, and even if no one was hurt, the traffic is slowed for hours. But one might just as easily imagine plenitude.

Like a cat locked up inside for days on end in a cottage with seven windows, as the night encroaches becoming more im-patient, crouching at one window and then the next, eyeing a street of conquests and howls, you are forever separated from the world by a series of veils as thin as battered summer screens. Stepping off the stoop, the humidity hits you, not envelops you. The body is a path, and you cannot lose the way. But you do.

A Question to Celan

If the admission were to require the dissolution
of the dream of the transmission of the solution,
and the admission were avoidable, and yet gnawed,
with the added possiblilty that only in the admission
would the guilt be born, the yield of apperception itself
the stolid clockwork self, would you then run to Rimbaud
and say with him that "I am the Other, I am being thought"?

The difficulty clearly lies in digging free the poem's
necessity from all other things in their foaming contingency.
Not to stand behind a work merely pointing out referents—it
can't be so simple—but to disappear into what you say, as
necessary as breath: but then you become the stream of your
speech, your mind cannot stand over what is made to watch
the path that speech directs towards the future, speech becomes
indistinguishable from a silence like a given thing: and while
silence provided the mouth from which thoughts and things
and all that which you spoke of arose, silence also provides
the broken space in rational speech that leaves us years later
drinking and *trinken* and *trinken* black milk and black milk from
a million seething photographic prints?

Attempt at Speech

A feeling not spoken   unspoken
throng of visions smoldering
in the fire, the fire's podium.
When bliss would have been possible
I dreamt of something minor
speaking from behind: such thoughts
should never come to pass to thought.
Forebodings of some other wording,
the "when" it might be possible to say
just now,   the rapture
behind despair. Yet here
there are only some perceptions
fixed within erotic wheelings, the tax
of the flesh upon itself and kind:
nothing else in sight or slumber but
the flesh flaunting its mineral braid.

*   *   *

Unspoken therefore unfelt
 I awoke: unspoken
hours had become some days.
Awareness divvies up
unawares in lust's defile:
half of what we are
    becomes submerged.
 It is the story of stupor all over again,
    of reason and desire,
of how they "fought" and cancelled so much
    of each other's energy out.

24

Rapt before a gripping tale.
Dreaming like your life
not only depended on it
but *was* it.
The fugitive red exposure of my habits
and the bricks above the imagined sky:
the incomplete mood just before
I catch on sleep in uneasy dark
this confused appointment with self
coming off and not coming off
as if *real* meant *vague*.

*   *   *

Let the kettle brim over this defile
wash away all I'd done to undo
the force of feeling. No more
bewilderment in the dark here forward
that will not *roar*:
the boundaries expanding
the water pouring over
what can be felt
yet perhaps be dammed   be
undammed later   the possibilities
that flood the chars   the embers
that will yet light
the podium in the eye of flame
speaker in the changing element
unity of the movement's song
all part of an impalpable crawling
over sight swept stone.

*   *   *

All must be at risk or what
is of a person hardens.
The adventure is total.
The mind is unmade.

25

Art of Expectation

Withdrawing from a single line what is tightly wound
within it: what it is I exalt, us in our nuptials sightless,
and less than sightless. Yet behind the screen of whatever
sibilance I choose to print, a naked wound, and the warmth of
what is naked, drawing us back to reality. To that of the gaze.

Pluto and this repertory were one once; now, a fountain
manages to spout from the ice. As if all were not in accord
with the scandal—weaving days out of straw, a pigmented love
not just there on the page but pointing towards you like a
pencil.

Not a book, but not distinct from a book. Reading, and
then seeing: desire and vision, rare overlap. Island of clarity.
Eyelid of clarity. The body a bending light, white light,
flesh light.

Until we make a dwelling in perception, until the percept
finds its dwelling in the dream, the seconds, those lights, only
a limbo of expectation. *The ideal always enters by the window.*

Between Perception

The objects now offered
were beyond any wearying:
a small coffee, whose caffeine flick
adds to the real. The phoenix,
the moment when the phoenix
rises from the ashes.
An ambulance siren reddening the morning
Then the ambulance in ashes too:
afterglow of the phoenix torch
A silence as if of touch.

*　*　*

Irritation at the heart of things
what you meant by the poem suddenly at a distance
And the sun no longer visible
not so much due to the sky—
Suddenly the poem at such a great distance—
as to the mind's turning away.

*　*　*

Despairing of the real.
Kids on the street,
burning potato chips:
my thinking at first it was a bird.
A moment of fright as the shriveled embers
struggle to flutter away.
Angry rush of air:
breath of the spirit into a walk without words.
In the mind that which suffocates

27

comes to nourish. That which is beyond thought
becomes a kind of bread.
The soul on fire: the illusion of souls.
        But the fire, real.
"Am I invisible?", a man in a rag
challenges from the corner, begging for change.
Abrupt, what we see, what we don't
its movement past, and always beyond.
My thought in my mouth
but thought out of breath.
Yes, yes, you *are* invisible
as everything real is made invisible
in the economy of need.

*   *   *

Awakening from some exhausting depth
to the proximity of the eye-lash
and a tentative perception of light.
Sweet, this sweat, desire yet combing
        the reaches of the body.
Her body asleep next to yours:
the fire, and the consciousness that survives it.
Mornings in such sleep, rapture dissolved,
stripped of identities, such as they were.
A cross-section of lust suddenly exposed to itself
as sated and done, yet desire still humming.
Life in the bed, eliding the facts.
Watching her sleep; others' awakenings.

*   *   *

The way the least visited museum
creaks when you enter. A long trip
for nothing, going two ways.
Stupor mundi: the faces in the subway.
Though the city sometimes arches its back,
blazes even, in the oblivion of its rebirth.
Then the distant veins tremble
as they circulate the living,

28

always the living, slowly towards their dens.
The city: a museum of unheard of contents.
Where handling the specimens is allowed
except that they handle you and you are one of them.
Excessive, the touching that goes on in this
imponderable vault. You lose yourself there.
You reel beneath the sheets as it roars under.
Stupor returns but in the form of joy.

* * *

Cemetery in the sun.
Before, only birds.
Then we come before the open grave:
she openly, uncontrollably, shakes.
Oh God, they're putting him into the ground.
Incredulous fact of her dead son,
hit by a truck in Galilee.
Maybe there's some mistake, I want to see his face,
she's cried. The face left unrecognizable,
    they'd examined his hand.
Oh God, they're putting him into the ground.
It closes you off, the cemetery gate,
leaves you alone in a world of mourning
over which the sun plays as if mourning were
an ordinary thing. Docile rows of polished cars,
an anguish running through the flesh:
the whiteness of the stones in a place
where others of your family have already been buried.
Yet a kind of indifference settles in
as if all this could be avoided by defiance
or good taste. Wondering about emotion,
how it vanishes only to then grab you by the chest.
His body, flown all the way back to Long Island,
        just for this ritual.
The sun filters through the hair of those erect.
The grass, green, and the breeze, softly blowing.
Seagulls: the proximity of the sea.
A silence as if of touch.

29

LIVING AND DYING
IN A SINGLE EXCHANGE

Poem

My love, I wish that we were both dead
    that way we could be together more often
    our skeltons tossed together in some common coffin
That staring deep into each other's eye-sockets
    stroking one another's foreheads
    and each other's ribs
There was no longer any need to write to you.

Report From Paris

after O.V. Milosz's "November Symphony"

The same door, yes, I'm sure of it, the same.
Here, at daybreak, a bird sits in the corridor
As pale as a corpse; then the silence anchors in
And you hear the tilting impassive noise of buckets
Overturning at the rampart.

Empty port, terrible terrible core!
And only the aegis of an abyss spitting up judgments.
Several metamorphoses, splinters of thoughts,
I take practically the same steps too!
Practically the same morning, cerebral, shining, veiled, shut.

And beyond these steps, an avenue, and beyond this avenue,
I'm speaking to you of a city on a scar, of the children
Of any person's personal degeneration, of a hatching limbo
And a low crumbling wall where the odor of cold rain drowses.
Old and oily, a leprous chimera comes seeking
        to transform you.

And I imagine you far off, clasped in pale violet enclosures.
And because I know only vacancy and concision I cannot hope
To imagine or know where or how to find you
        among those enclosures.
As with this step, damp with the echo of my effigy.
As with these eyes, unable to overcome their lids.

The same steps, the same faces: and toward midday people will
        come here and shuffle about
Who I think will never know each other and who can be
        faulted only for this:
That they must dress and sometimes riot, lovelessly
And without benefit of light, each plotting, within earshot
Of the other, when the other snaps shut with resignation.

The Beautiful American Word "Sure"

after O.V. Milosz's "The Scale"

Bending into this
imposing symmetrical progression
the things done that year
sometimes succeed,
around June, at dawn,
in half-opening
into two or three
stuttered words,
which echo forth
brilliant fading echoes
on the steps
and in the hallways
of homes,
or uttered elsewhere,
fade in the pale
echoless interiors of cars.

I have stared at the back
of a head for hours,
passing over fiery highways!
Yet just for a moment, before,
maybe you'd felt your eyes
touched by frenzy,
insuppressible, impulsive,
almost senseless,
as confused as the odor
of rain and resolution.
Now, as with a camera,
its cartridge unpacked,
the contents as yet undeveloped,

clear and yet faint,
an indistinct image of yourself
is held in the mind.
And caught in the synapse
of an intolerable conjecture,
a vague unbearable moon,
interior and distant,
one of those enriching
uncatalogued surfaces,
rousing in us.

"Too far gone on thought to ever"...
to ever scent anything
but bright disorder
in the morning
and in the consciousness of the morning,
a progress in chaos
as sometimes one hopes.
And if maybe it's only
the illusion of waking
and these silent waters aren't
"legitimized by any empiricism,"
then at least out the same window
the faceless limit, the multitude
that shouldn't be softened,
the chances for brutality,
also are not real.

"A child closes his hand
around the neck
of a trembling sparrow
flown too soon from its nest,"
and yes, you wonder why
they do it
and what can remain after.
It contradicts and it does not contradict,
as when you were voracious,
a present anticipating a change
for the better,
insisting upon yourself
as you were.

The Garden

The garden hinges on the sea.
Mutable garden, garden further on, blindness to garden.
I try to catch a glimpse of what is
and of what is of necessity departing,
to think of the birds twittering in the flesh.
But the peace here comes to be the same
as the slackening in the rope
when the ferry commences to depart.
And in this inattentive torpor
I've allowed my love's head to empty,
and an empty bird falls back from the others,
and hovers, hovers over the bosom of the spoken;
but she's not fallen out of time; and I,
"I" further on, am myself like a sensation,
and like that transcendent thing that's throbbing so.
What then is this anxiety that is always coming along,
causing who knows what in me?

December

1

I've always been ignorant, embedded at the beginning
In a sort of sponge, of location and time, knowing little,
But that it was dark there and seemingly timeless, and that
Now I hold within me something that burns with a low fire
    from that time.

2

One toils, in reflection, for one is condemned, however frail,
    to live long.
I've already tasted a little bit the terrible obscurity of life,
The fish in the pitiless movements of the body's lakes.
I have the feeling most of my life will be spent alone.

3

And always the consciousness of the image of the thing
    one must one day become:
My small interrogation suddenly turned into a tiny
    mass of beliefs,
Wandering about some place under a heavy load of fear,
Bitter blind spots hidden beneath the whitened bald spots!

4

I do not know why it died, but as it did, did it not, like a kiss,
Bequeath all its fiery cradled colors to my thoughts and lips?
Oh God, it's a mother one cannot express, and afflicted
    in this way,
One jokes, but suffers, struggles speechlessly
    in the tissued darkness.

5

I know of course that it is speaking and understanding that are
    throttled in us.
But that superseded thought of life and the deadly future,
    for all of us,
That's what I find unbearable. "It's really the panic of an
insect within me,
And an insect's cry deep within me, beneath the heart's ashes."

I, It

It explores with such an ephemeral touch these things
initiated in order to espouse the ephemeral
that when his hand is obliged to draw back and choose
the place where this art will redden
it can only say: "this variation is not my vision."
It has put a piece of the other in all the other regions;
that taught him space, space sleekened and came closer;
and in his memory, from before,
fingers were held inside his mouth and pacified its cries,
as in the distinct experience of a thing.

Pure passivities move in all my accounts of that time,
    and leaning
over the latent one hears a crude answer, a map of voices,
the noises of palpitation and circumstance, of hardened speech.
Lend it a hand; think harder for example;
and imperious and desultory, say what?
"The whole relationship between mind and body,
We will bury it tomorrow?"
"The depths of the imaginary are like fossils
drawn into participation,
while the two halves of an orange form a whole?"
"First you were a direction, later your eyes grew,
and you became eyes?"
Absurd, absurd, of course, and if by the same token
they were to set off a place for these two hands
and unite there also all that was of my perception,
that space would conclude by covering all.
But I have no body, only certain limitations,
which makes it better;
what more contradicts the massive, the moving,
stones, landmarks, signs?

"Yet never can it be said he renounced
the tangible or even crisscrossed it."
Rather, I am eating alone, barely alive,
in the fever of these tufts.
My nudity happens to save me, thought not by design.
I have stamped upon my literal experience with such fecundity
yet it is other conversation that has formed my person
and this flesh remains what it was,
a chaos proud of its order, punctuated and rushing.
A gaze that bleats in the light,
a passive subject in the dark:
in this succession of unfixed interiors I have been beating up
the brute world by use of an alleged sense
which instead consumes myself and pierces my dimensions.

Eight Variations on a Stranger

after O.V. Milosz's "L' Etrangère"

1

I know only the warmth of my motives, have dreamed
    them up,
Most tangibly been forced to dream.
You'll see my face in the rains coursing brilliance,
I know nothing of my motives, nor do I wish to.

2

You sputter of remote thresholds, fiery—
Never will I pass through them
Or hear their names with full understanding.
I've watched August happen,
Watched things drift this close to fall.

3

You are distant, alien—you are
A bastille of sun,
A drizzle—historical, futural—this side of the walls
Flung along the coastline between earth and air.

4

This—this day: a summer's day under the light,
The citizens banished into their strange freedoms;
This is where you will curb me too after all the talk,
Without any explanation of how I am to continue.

5

Like a fated place the dying city
Chuckles with fire and bereavement.
Like a great nude forest the live city
Chuckles with rain and reflected fire—

6

A ray of old sunlight
Bending less than that oar where sadness meets joy.
Leave me one thing—ignorance of those ways
In which chance has crushed your architecture into me.

7

Circuitous work, living and dying in a single exchange!
One might just as well say you've never laid words on me,
That my vaults in the streets have never brought echoes,
That my pale rationality is but a fragment of oblivion.

8

In some region of gold and eagerness,
In the ambivalent warmth of a house of furs,
Amongst tables and talk,
We will meet once, will you remember?

REAWAKENING

Awaiting Validation

In some far recess, it is all known already, before you
begin to make things emerge. But this is not to say that some
mythical private space is enough in itself, or that reflection
alone is an antidote. No, unfortunately, it is unavoidable,
movement is in some sense necessary and inevitable, anyway.
Nor can this transformation be an imagined one, motions
made in dreams, for the very screen these dreams flit across
has yet to be validated. Now, since I have never acted or
thought of my own accord, and yet walk and think, without
ever consulting what is actual or public, I am merely the
composite of my dreams. Hence, as of this date, I am invalid
or, better yet, awaiting validation. Pretty certain that
everything I know, and feed from, and distribute, has been
tricked into light or scraped from the edges of my veins with
the edge of a card, nervously aware that this is not enough, I
watched an apple tree fill with lightly glowing pink sap, as if it
were thoroughly nourished by its own limbs; and I realized
how far apart in recent years the trees and I had grown. Once
our roots had intertwined together in a mutual soil, and
neither one of us would move all day, except insofar as the
wind brushed against its leaves, the hairs on my toes. We
would lie in the bush together, all men saw of me were my
feet, my head and torso were buried that deeply in its lap.
That much I remember. But beyond that, I remember
little, for instance the precise way the leaves would flutter in a
passing breeze is beyond my recollection, not only because my
eyes had not yet been dislodged but also because, subsequently,
the silts dug loose have all but covered these things up. My
eyes have been dislodged for quite some time now, however,
and I fear they desire to branch out a little themselves. How
can one possibly imagine into what skies they will arch their
irises? Who can know how long the boughs will maintain the

weight of the events the eyes bring back? Who can know or imagine if the card I cut with will ever drop from my hand, or if that far recess, so imminent too, will ever reveal itself?

The lids like mouths only recently savored the tree, the lonely sockets already demand new ornamentations, and thirst for wells. Soon, perhaps, the metamorphosis will be complete, and my eyes will have been changed from moths into stones, or apples.

Vulva Myth

after W.S.' "Seventy Years Later"

for Trisha

It is an illusion that we ever desired,
That we ever dived among the folds of the belly
Or splayed ourselves out in a fussing of flesh.

Even our moistures, their tastes, no longer tempt.
The lusts erected in the bed have reached their close.
They never were... The harmonic curves on curves

Were not, are not, could never have been.
There was nothing to be pleasured.
No dance of the torso was ever held

Nor spoken of afterwards, greedily.
The full globes reacting to the tip
Of each finger could only have been

Dead ends, a caressing of one ousted shape
Against another, the very anithesis of
The principle proposed between the legs—

That thighs conceal a voluptuous breeze,
Or underthings in their animal warmth
A luxuriance so desired that once unveiled

The vulva, however unreal, quivered,
That the sexes came and soldered, an exclaiming
Of bright cries, on the verge of satisfied,

49

In a wave of sight and sweat. The glaring,
The hiking up, these were not desire,
Incessant burning formed no wet pyre,

Just as this, in the aftermath, is not life.

Desire

The Coursing

Sorrows, cloistered in the soul.
Pouring out of offices, crowds of souls in pain,
their lurch and thrash in the nets of becoming.
An inquisitrix of light arcs down the sidewalk,
stabbing the scene with pleasure, lashing at the avenue.
Caught in an exquisite midstep, illusion
and its necessity, Necessity's indifferent coursing,
the fountain and the contents of the fountain,
their pink indifferent foaming.
"How should we ever go on except for desire,
or more, except that desire were disproportionate
to its means, its object, and, at last, to anything here?"

Opening

Orifice where the light forges itself:
soft "V", from which I'm never coming out.
Her naked lips pressed back, what fascinates
her sex, the lapping of my tongue. Irony withers
when all is wet, what flows from its collapse:
giddiness of affirmation free from Babel
the glow there like the glowing of the excited silver moon
the words regaining their hunger for the infinite.
All else only imagination's bender after hours,
aspiration giving way to rhetorical response.
Bound within desire's run, the sensation of "no":
and now of "yes". Closer to the center the tires screech.
Written naked in its road a cage that stands in space.
As with this glossy fountain, gleaming in the sun.
Where the heart had its accident, will again.
What begins in joy ends before joy's begun.

Beauty

It begins with sight, advances outward.
Delicate ocean water, mermaids on the waves.
What is fluid in her motions, in the fluid of her come.
Or the movement of a weeping willow
where another rhythm rules: the pond
where the city masquerades as nature. A voice
among the voices to which the voice responds.
Solitude expressing itself in an expressive overflow.
Lust, for control, sucking, to be comforted.
What gleams of desire, and what hisses
of desire. *The cache of the crotch.*
Where words would flag in the absence of first flesh,
an alphabet of pubic curls. Beautiful,
the way she glows, when I call her beautiful.
To say her name would be to name her.
Except she makes me pass from what
would limit to repose in what she is.
In what is not: a single coursing of the soul.
A heightened sense that time and desire
can coincide, indeed. Pressing against
her breasts away from time.
Already rushing away, that sense,
as quickly as will the light.

*

The most fantastic movement of the mind
is self-forgetfulness, still rich with thought:
in a nutshell, tenderness. These are the hands
that carry out the text at hand.
With its marvelous, its private
Sensitivities, the sexual fruit responds.

An emotion that speaks in buoyant gold.
How the body awakens to its vaster vision.
Graceful movements, as with a flipper:
some great half-fish of feeling
undulating in the light-filled morning.
Nothing moves. A comb lies on a wicker trunk.
Reality is what you look for here, not dreams' debris.
As if the clarity of the features of the woman's face
should stamp the room as well. Always delight before
darkness, or darkness before delight, or maybe not,
this unpredictability causing you a rapturous suspense.
It begins in sight, the green waves
lapping at your sides. A feeling
that fixes you with a transfixing look.
Deep blue eyes in a sonorous key.
A map of Central Park, a room
that sways in pine. Plenitude of things,
their sources elsewhere. The sensation of reflection,
sudden presencing of what was unseen before.
With that, a new measure. Electrical things
all turned off, but thought electric.
Each particular, aroused.
And no prohibitions.

Form

An immediacy of mind,
a chaos built of stones;
a foyer, of astonishing brilliance.

And a limousine, pulling out of the familiar.

I belonged to the far off parapet
                and was part of it
part of the cage of fire on the limo's dashboard.

An instant, a movement,
a nerve that doesn't stand a chance

to order the chaos yet leave the astonishment blaze.

Meditation

1

God and all his simulacra
were part of our physiology,

part of the rapture of meditation
whose whalebrow lies lustrous here,

the protuberance of Manhattan reascending
into sight as if by sway of light;

we are t-shirts, boots, forelocks,
the besouled custodians

of a dark-skinned skyscraper
equivalent to the night.

Not the beached and denuded sea-beast,
nor a species bound for extinction;

Not a monster with a heart
but the heart, that monster;

Not everything is appointed
and it is good that this island was not appointed

Yet still arrives,
The exactitude of form

In the water,
the hugeness of the unseen beneath.

To be swallowed up
by a city's invisible contingencies,

The specifically contingent ecstasy of
the city as the island as the fish,

A spawning awareness of something
larger than one's own decline:

Yet this ecstatic equation—the denizen
as Jonah as escapee but only from himself—

Is not intelligible to the escapee denizen,
and the custodianship of the contingent

Remains unfelt. God and all his simulacra
lead us to bed. Necessity is still sought.

*An impenetrable self-reference
locks the only door.*

The city too resubmerges . . .
it is as if with God's cooling

All that which suffered the creation
were now speaking the first words of nothingness,

An invisible parlance of visible things
sealing the obscurity of the spoken

Within the obscurity of each skin—
as if the half-lit buildings of this zone

In their interiors encircled only
eyeless nomads impassioning each other,

Simulacrum realizing itself,
struggling together, absolute in tenderness.

2

In the face of God's repose,
God was inflamed:
that was the God of both
repose and flame.
A God that for the first time
glimpsed itself, but mistook
itself for another (what other
would God imagine himself to be?)
Or, dimly conscious of its error,
the divine denial of a God
unwilling to see itself
as the source of an
elegance of words
but a world in ruins.

What is, cannot be,
cries out to be burned away.
God *is* what cries out,
and the anger that falls
upon that cry.
Sky raging at the sky

In lightning strokes:
self-flagellating spirit,
sparked by the eye
to strike at itself.

Like what happens
at the limits of the self
at the moment we choose
not to recognize them.

Like boundaries of body,
categories of thought,
confounded by speech,
the lovers lie entwined
at the heart of God's lash.

Pause: even patience
is delirium, or else we would not
conceive of each hour as *waiting*.
As waiting for the next God.

3

The vision of the eye impaired
not by its own deficiency
or by any real obstacle
but by a deficiency in what *can* be seen.

This is the further storm.

The death not of the subject
but of the object.

The world beyond
out to lunch.

      Static yet supple tree
ecstatic in the sun:
reality and its report.
The rushing loins of light.
As if a proof of life.

Misleading headline:
the motorcade of the imagination
brought all traffic to a stop.
I was there, and I can say:
nothing in that stream abated.

Yet until the voice
      makes the separation
a testament to beauty
      and a misleading headline
read as one——

The voice not of God
    but of whoever it is
found lying amid the rubble
    not far from the tree,

A voice that does not say a thing
    but whose mythical presence
shapes the difference,
    grounds each word.
Your own voice.
    Your own silence.
Amid the rubble of good and evil.

4

On certain mornings it brings no joy to imagine the stringy,
golden light of afternoon. As if to look to the sun were to
realize that the sun is a vestige: the shadow thrown off by a
sculpture is more the light of man.

At work in the hand, then, the generative activity behind
everything visible.

Myth, myth remaking noon: the sculpture is free, we are
molded. Marble becomes flesh, we become stone. *The struggle of
the physical bodies to define themselves out of the stone within which
they are still held bound.* Those bodies, toiling desperately,
desperation in their eyes. The half-lit towers immobile on the
shore.

It happens too that sculpture comes back to grapple with our
unpolished hands. Like us it wants to be the Other; in being
made, desire flowed from us to it, until it is what we desire,
until it desires. Of course it desires: it is our creation, made in
our image. And almost as we might have dreamt it, the
sculpture rushes towards us. We look up at it, catch at it with
whatever tricks of matter lie at hand.

The city is such a stunt, made from thought though sculpted in
thoughtlessness. The whirl of a weather helicopter, the clawfoot
of a building, the hammering in the street as the street is
hammered out: when to such movements we awake, we awake
within the very object that we seek.

Not to the effigy in the mirror, charred black from fire and
deja vu.

Not as a point of light without a form, a fear upon the pillow
on the bed.

But as participants in its being.

5

Before sorrow
it came
to fire summer

Before seasons
it *was* fire

Without it
a sleep as deep
as total eclipse.

A rapture of meditation
no longer recognizable in the light of day:

Plunge bravely, then, into each day's generation.

60

GNOSIS PRESS

Alternate Currents

Victoria Andreyeva, *Dream of the Firmament,* poems. A bilingual edition. Translated from Russian by **Richard McKane.**

Stephen Sartarelli, *Grievances and Other Poems.*

Thomas Epstein, *Man and a Half,* fiction.

Gregory Kapelyan, *Obsidian Idol,* fiction.

Arkady Rovner, *The King's Visit,* a novel.

Arkady Rovner and **Victoria Andreyeva,** *Tchaadayev,* a play.